Every new generation of children is enthralled by the famous stories in our Well-loved Tales series. Younger ones love to have the story read to them. Older children will enjoy the exciting stories in an easy-to-

WELL-LOVED TALES

The Pied Piper of Hamelin

retold for easy reading
by ROSE IMPEY
illustrated by RICHARD HOOK

Ladybird Books

Once upon a time, and this was a long time ago, the people of Hamelin were not very happy. And they had good reason. Their town was over-run with rats. They were everywhere, hundreds and thousands of them, and the numbers were growing by the day. They found their way into every barn, every store-room, every house and every cupboard.

Oh, they were greedy rats. They ate all the corn which was stored for the winter. They ate the cheese as fast as it was made. The fruit was no sooner picked than it was gobbled up by the rats. They drank the milk from the buckets. They supped the wine and all the beer in the barrels. Soon there was little food or drink left for the people of the town. The place was hardly worth living in.

Mothers had to keep watch over their children and the babies in their cradles. They dared not take their eyes off the food cooking for the evening meal. If they did, some big, bold rat would come along and eat up all the food. It would lick the pots clean, leaving never a taste for the hungry family. Things were in a bad state.

As if that wasn't bad enough, the noise was deafening. Throughout the town there was a shrieking and a squeaking, a hurrying and a scurrying. It would have made your head ache. By day the people couldn't hear themselves speak, and by night they hardly had a wink of sleep.

I suppose you are wondering why the people of Hamelin didn't set their cats and dogs to rid the town of rats. Well, they did. The fights were tremendous. But, in the end, the rats were too much and too many for the poor cats and dogs, which were driven away into the countryside, too scared to come home.

Soon the people were at their wits' end, and so they marched in a crowd to the Town Hall. They banged on the heavy, wooden door and demanded to speak to the Mayor.

When he appeared, the people were so angry, they shook their fists at him.

“We have had enough of sharing our town and our food with rats. You must do something about it. If you don’t find a way to get rid of these pests, we will find a new Mayor.”

And they turned around and walked back to their homes, muttering and grumbling to each other.

So that was how it was. The Mayor had to find a way out of this problem or he had to find a new job. Now this Mayor thought himself no end of a fine fellow. He was a greedy man, but he

was also quite clever. He decided to offer a reward to anyone who could rid the town of rats. One thousand guilders he promised, which was a lot of money, I can tell you. And it was far more than the Mayor really had.

Rat-catchers came from all over Germany. They tried every way they knew to catch those rats. They netted them and trapped them. They poisoned them and

smoked them out of their holes. But whatever they tried there seemed to be more rats than ever, cocking their tails and pricking their whiskers.

Then, one day, when the Mayor had almost given up hope, a stranger appeared in the town. He made his way to the Town Hall and asked to see the Mayor.

Now, this was a strange fellow. He was tall and thin, and his face was twisted into a mocking smile. His eyes were sharp and bright as a bird's. They danced as he spoke.

But most strange of all were his clothes. He wore a long, ragged gown, with wide sleeves reaching almost to the ground. One half was yellow and the other half was red.

Around his waist, he wore a leather belt, into which was tucked a long, thin pipe. It was carved all around with mysterious signs and markings. His cap had long ears, with bells that jingled when he moved.

The Mayor and his Council had never seen anyone like the stranger before. They couldn't imagine what the man had come for. The Mayor would have liked to turn him away, but there was

something about the stranger which frightened him.

"What do you want with me?" asked the Mayor.

"I am called the Pied Piper," said the man. "I have come to rid your town of rats, and to earn the one thousand guilders, your Honour!" He gave a bow and his lips wore that odd smile, as if he were enjoying a joke.

"If you can do as you say, you shall have the thousand guilders, and that is a promise. But what makes you think you can succeed when all the others have failed?" asked the Mayor.

The Piper smiled again.

"The music I play, none can resist."

Then he turned and left the Hall and walked into the main street. There, he laid his pipe lightly to his lips and a shrill tune was heard all over the town. As each note was carried further and further on the air, things began to happen. First you could hear a rumbling

and grumbling, as if an army was on the move. Then a bustling and rustling, then a creaking and squeaking, as the rats began to pour out of the houses. They came from windows and doors, from attics and cellars, from every corner and hidy-hole.

There were rats of every kind. Great rats and small rats, black rats and grey rats. There were sharp and quick ones, slow unfit ones. Fathers, mothers, sisters,

brothers, all came pouring forth. Soon the Piper was surrounded by them. As night began to fall he moved along the street and the rats surged after him.

He led them, at a steady pace, out of the town until he reached the wide River Weser. Still playing his pipe, he stepped into a boat and sailed off towards deep

water. With an everlasting SPLASH! the rats plunged into the dark river. There they drowned, every last one of them.

Then there was much rejoicing in the town of Hamelin. The happy people rang the church bells, and danced and sang. They blocked off the holes and pulled down the nests. They repaired all the damage until there wasn't a trace of a rat to be found. Soon it seemed as if the rats of Hamelin had never been.

The Mayor was pleased with himself. The townspeople were pleased with him, too. He felt that he deserved a new cloak and a new gold chain, as a little reward. After all, it was thanks to his idea that the town had been rid of the rats. He decided to give a dinner for his

friends, to celebrate their good fortune. But there was one person who was not invited. Who was that? You might well ask! In all their excitement, they had forgotten the Pied Piper. Most of all they had forgotten the one thousand guilders, which he had been promised.

As the Mayor and his friends were sitting down to enjoy their feast there was a loud knock at the door. It was the Pied Piper. He had come for his money.

But the money wasn't there. The Mayor had spent most of it. He stood in his new cloak, wearing his new gold chain, with his friends all around him. He was in a real fix.

"Now what shall I do?" thought the Mayor. "I haven't got that much money and there is nothing I can do about it. One thousand guilders just for playing a tune! The man must think I am mad to pay such a price."

"You will have to be satisfied with fifty guilders," he told the Piper. Which was true; it was all that was left.

Well, the Piper was not a man to stand this kind of nonsense. "One thousand guilders you promised, and if I were you I would pay up quickly. For I can play many kinds of tunes, as you may find to your cost, my fine friend."

Now that made the Mayor angry.

"You dare to threaten me! You strolling vagabond! Fifty guilders is all you will get. Take it or leave it. The rats are dead and gone, so do your worst."

“Very well,” said the Piper, and he smiled his twisted smile. Once more he stepped into the street and laid his pipe lightly to his lips. This time a very different tune came forth.

It was a gentle sound of laughter and happiness. It seemed to tell wonderful stories, which made the listener strain forward for fear of missing one note. It was music which made you want to dance and follow on wherever it led.

When the children of Hamelin heard it they stopped what they were doing and rushed out. They came running and laughing from playroom and schoolroom, from nursery and workshop. Every child in the town was drawn on by the marvellous music of the magic pipe.

The townspeople stood by and watched as their children held hands and flocked to join the happy crowd. Their cheeks glowed and their eyes sparkled as they listened to the tales the music told. They ran behind the Piper as he made his way along the street and out of the town. Each child followed at his own speed. The quick ones kept close by his heels but the little lame boy came slowly behind. The people tried to call them back but the children could only hear the music of the Pied Piper.

This time, when he reached the River Weser, the Piper crossed by the wide wooden bridge. The townspeople sighed with relief to see their children safe on the other side. They felt sure the children would soon be tired and make their way

home. Yet the Piper led them on. The soft notes of his music seemed to float in and out of the trees as they passed through a wood. The children skipped and danced among the tall oak and beech trees.

At last they came to a steep hill-side. "Now he must stop," the people thought. "He can never lead the children across those hills." But they had no idea of the Piper's power. All at once an opening appeared, leading deep into the hill-side. The Piper led the way

into a wide cave and the children followed, still skipping and dancing. When all but one were inside, the cave closed up with a slam, like the heavy closing of an oak door. Not a sign remained of the cave or the opening. It was as if it had never been.

Just one child remained, the little lame boy. Unable to keep up with his friends, he had been left behind. He searched and searched but he could find no way through the solid rock. At last he returned

home, sad and disappointed. The people came running to meet him. He told how the music had promised to lead the children to a wonderful place and how happily they had followed it.

From time to time the little boy returned to the spot, far from the town, where he could sometimes hear the strange music. It seemed to come from within the hills, but faintly, as if it had travelled a long distance. The music was so sweet that he longed to follow it, but there was no way through. It was many years before the sound of children's happy voices was heard again in Hamelin town.